Sion's Misfortune

Chen Jiafei | Wang Ran

A long time ago, in an ancient kingdom along the Great Wall of China, there lived a man named Sion.

Sion was a fortune-teller, and an excellent one at that. Everyone in his little town went to him with questions about their futures, and he was never wrong.

One day, when Sion's horse was grazing, it unknowingly galloped across the border into the neighboring kingdom. The two kingdoms had been at war for many years, and so no one was allowed to cross over to bring it back home.

"Oh, no! You will never see your poor horse again, Sion!" wailed all his friends and relatives.

Pity flooded in for Sion from everyone, but to their surprise, he just smiled and said, "For all you know, this might be a good thing."

And just as he had predicted, an extraordinary thing happened days later. Sion's horse came back safe and sound but it was not alone! Behind it came several wild horses. They were strong and muscular, with gleaming coats and glossy manes.

Sion's friends were astonished, but also quite frightened. They went to congratulate him on the return of his precious horse and asked, "What will you do about all these wild horses, Sion? You know nothing about their nature."

Once again, they were baffled by his reply. "This might actually be a good thing," said Sion. Nobody could understand why he would say such a thing, and they hurried away when one of the horses neighed menacingly. "He's in for some trouble," they whispered to each other.

Several weeks went by. Sion's son, who had always been rather shy, grew very fond of the horses. His father was delighted to see how adventurous they'd made his otherwise timid son. One day, when Sion's son was riding one of the wild horses, he fell off and broke his leg.

Sion's son lay in bed in great pain, with his leg in a thick cast.

He was told he would
not be able to walk at all
for the next few weeks.

All of Sion's friends and neighbors
clicked their tongues in sympathy.
"Poor young lad!" they said.
"Such rotten luck!"

They were aghast when Sion chuckled,
"This could be a very good thing!"
They thought it was such a silly thing
for a wise man to keep saying, and
that perhaps he was not thinking
clearly any longer.

The following morning, the townspeople were
in for a great shock. Their kingdom faced an
unexpected attack by the neighboring kingdom.

The elders in the town grew tense as they received news that all young people would be drafted into the army to defend their soil.

The battle lasted nearly a month. It was a brutal fight.

And by the time it ended, thousands had lost their lives.

But Sion's son remained safe at home the whole time, for he could not possibly be sent off to war with an injured leg.

And at long last, the people of Sion's town finally understood...

... that misfortune could indeed be a blessing!

Chen Jiafei got her bachelor's degree in Nanjing University, and a master's at Peking University. She is now pursuing many literary adventures of her own. She believes that telling stories is the best way to remember who you love.

Wang Ran is a graphic designer and illustrator with several published books. She has won many awards for her work, and her favorite painting tools are Chinese ink and paper.

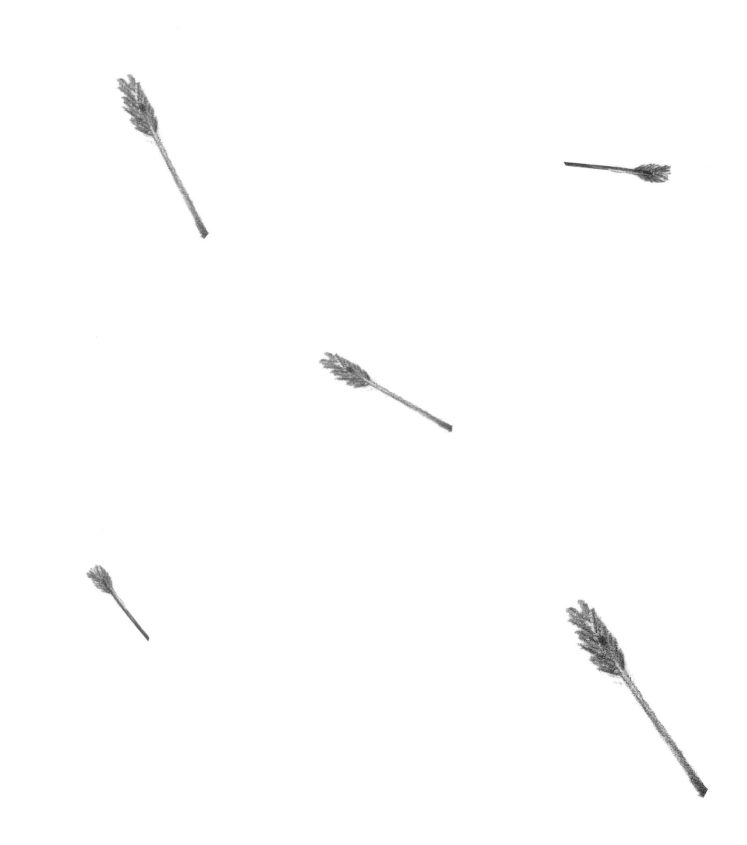

Sion's Misfortune

First published 2017 by Jiangsu Fine Arts Publishing House
First U.S. Print July 2019
First Print India

Text: Chen Jiafei
Illustrations: Wang Ran

Karadi Tales Company Pvt. Ltd. 3A Dev Regency,
11 First Main Road, Gandhinagar, Adyar, Chennai 600020.
Tel.: +91-44-42054243 | email: contact@karaditales.com
www.karaditales.com

ISBN: 978-81-9365-425-5

Distributed in the United States by Consortium Book Sales & Distribution
www.cbsd.com
Cataloging - in - Publication information:
Jiafei, Chen
Sion's Misfortune / Chen Jiafei; illustrated by Wang Ran
p.36; color illustrations; 24.5 x 24 cm.

JUV000000 JUVENILE FICTION / General
JUV074000 JUVENILE FICTION / Diversity & Multicultural
JUV012040 JUVENILE FICTION / Fairy Tales & Folklore / Adaptations
JUV030020 JUVENILE FICTION / People & Places / Asia